EGMONT
We bring stories to life

First published in Great Britain in 2015 by Egmont UK Limited,
The Yellow Building, 1 Nicholas Road, London W11 4AN.

Writer: Kate Graham
Designer: Andrea Philpots

© 2015 Disney Enterprises, Inc.

The movie THE PRINCESS AND THE FROG copyright © 2009 Disney,
inspired in part by the book THE FROG PRINCESS by E. D. Baker
copyright © 2002, published by Bloomsbury Publishing, Inc.

ISBN 978 1 4052 7793 8
60296/1
Printed in Italy

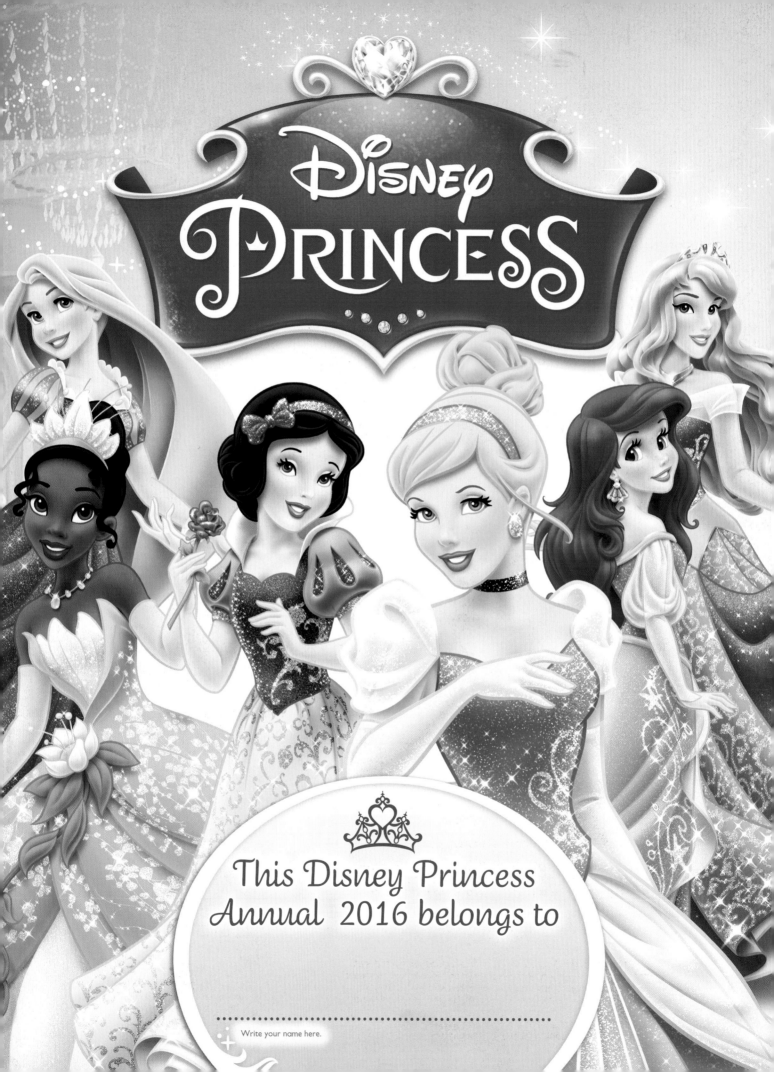

Disney PRINCESS

This Disney Princess
Annual 2016 belongs to

....
Write your name here.

DISNEY PRINCESS

All About ... Cinderella

🍎 **Cinderella is special because:** she is gracious, beautiful, gentle and hard-working. Like a true princess, Cinderella holds onto her dreams.

🍎 **Cinderella's special friends:** Jaq and Gus (the mice), Fairy Godmother and small birds.

🍎 **Cinderella's special love:** Prince Charming.

🍎 **A special moment in Cinderella's story:** when Fairy Godmother waves her magic wand and turns a pumpkin into a coach, the mice into horses and Cinderella's rag dress into a ballgown with glass slippers. Now Cinderella can go to the Royal Ball!

8

Cinderella's friends cheered
her up when her stepsisters were mean.
Draw a picture here of someone
who makes you feel happy.

"They can't order me
to stop dreaming."

Cinderella

Garden Games

Cinderella and Prince Charming are playing with their friends in the palace garden. Join in the fun!

1 Match all of Cinderella's friends to their shadow.

a

b

Gus

c

d

e

Prince Charming

Bruno

Lucifer

Jaq

2 Garden Quiz

Lucifer is a dog.

TRUE ♡   FALSE ♥

Cinderella is wearing a blue dress.

TRUE ♥   FALSE ♡

The mice have flowers for Cinderella.

TRUE ♡   FALSE ♥

11

Answers on page 66.

Where's my Ballgown?

1 Today the kingdom was buzzing with excitement because of the Grand Charity ball. The dress Cinderella chose for the evening was blue with pink roses embroidered on it.

2 Just after Cinderella left her room, Anastasia passed by and noticed the beautiful ballgown. It was much prettier than her own dress for the ball.

3 Anastasia loved the dress so much, she took it to her own room! But Jaq and Gus were watching …

4 With the help of their friends, they took the dress. "To Cinderelly's room!" said Gus, racing down the hall.

5 But unfortunately, Cinderella's friends ran into Lucifer. The birds and mice quickly scattered, leaving the ballgown draped across the stairs.

6 Lucifer curled up in front of the stairs and yawned. "He looks like he is going to take one of his long, long naps!" said Jaq. "Now we can't bring Cinderelly her dress," said Gus, sadly.

7 A little later, the Fairy Godmother was looking for Cinderella. When she saw the beautiful dress by the stairs, she was confused. "A ballgown belongs in a ballroom," she thought.

8 So she hung Cinderella's ballgown up in the ballroom.

9 Meanwhile, Anastasia felt bad and admitted to Cinderella she had taken her dress. But when they went into Anastasia's room, the ballgown wasn't there!

10 Then, Gus and Jaq arrived. They explained what had happened after they tried to return her dress but now it wasn't on the stairs where they left it.

11 At the same time, the Prince was passing by the ballroom and noticed Cinderella's dress. "This shouldn't be here," he thought, so he took it back to Cinderella's room.

12 Cinderella was still searching for her dress. The Fairy Godmother admitted that she had put it in the ballroom but when they got there, the dress was missing!

13 "I'll just have to wear an old dress," said Cinderella sadly, as she walked back to her room. When she went inside, the beautiful dress was hanging on her coat stand – just where she had left it!

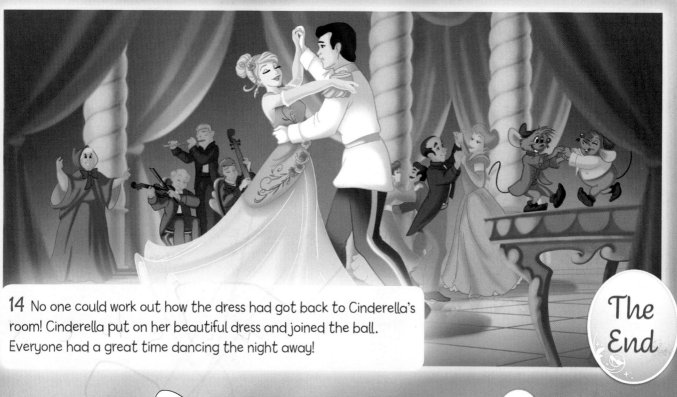

14 No one could work out how the dress had got back to Cinderella's room! Cinderella put on her beautiful dress and joined the ball. Everyone had a great time dancing the night away!

The End

Colour in Cinderella's new shoes so they match her ballgown.

15

I Believe ...

Use the picture code below to work out Cinderella's secret message. Write the letters below each picture.

Code

c e h
i m o r
s t u w

w i s h e s

c o m e

t r u e

Answer on page 66.

Graceful Cinderella

Colour in Cinderella – and be sure to use a
beautiful blue for her dress!

All About ... Rapunzel

✳ Rapunzel is special because: she is sweet, artistic, brave and passionate. Most importantly, Rapunzel always follows her heart.

✳ Rapunzel's special friends: Pascal (a cute chameleon) and Maximus (a horse).

✳ Rapunzel's special love: Flynn Rider.

✳ A special moment in Rapunzel's story: when Flynn takes Rapunzel out to the middle of the harbour in a rowing boat so that she can watch the beautiful floating lanterns in the night sky.

Are you artistic like Rapunzel?
Decorate this lantern with patterns,
then colour it in so it's fit for a princess!

"Sometimes you have to face your
deepest fears in order to make your
wildest dreams come true."

Rapunzel

19

Bunny Friend

Rapunzel has made friends with this sweet
and cuddly bunny since escaping from the tower.

1

How many
butterflies can
you see? Write the
number here.

2

Can you
find Pascal?

3

Follow the trail
to find some
food for bunny.

Answers on page 66.

Cute Pascal!

Pascal is always by Rapunzel's side. As long as she's happy, he is too!

a

b

c

d

1

These pictures of Rapunzel and Pascal look the same, but one is different. Which one is it?

2

Trace the letters to find out who loves Rapunzel.

Pascal

Answers on page 66.

Long Lost Hair

Rapunzel's long hair was amazing, but sometimes it got her into trouble, too!

After Flynn rescued Rapunzel from the tower, he cut off her long, golden hair to save her. It turned brown instantly and lost its healing power, but Rapunzel was finally free!

With her new short hair, Rapunzel found some things easier. She could climb trees without getting her hair tangled in the branches. She could ride Max without having to hold up her long hair.

But sometimes Rapunzel missed her long, golden hair ... like when Rapunzel and Flynn were picking berries and Flynn got stuck on the side of a steep ravine.

"I'll throw down my hair," said Rapunzel, before remembering that it was too short. Instead, Max and Pascal came to Flynn's rescue.

Another day, Rapunzel watched as the village girls decorated their long braids with flowers. Her brown hair wasn't long enough to make a braid to stick flowers in.

Then there was the time when Rapunzel went to heal Max's injured leg with her short, brown hair. She had forgotten that her hair no longer had magic powers. "Oh, I miss all the things I could do with my long hair!" Rapunzel told Flynn.

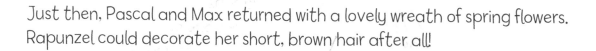

"Yes, but sometimes it caused trouble," replied Flynn. "Like when we were dancing and your hair knocked everything off the table. And what about when Pascal got lost in your hair?" he added.

"That was a HUGE mess," said Rapunzel. "By the way, where is Pascal now? And Max?"

Just then, Pascal and Max returned with a lovely wreath of spring flowers. Rapunzel could decorate her short, brown hair after all!

"You're so sweet," she said. "I love my short, brown hair and I love being free, but what I love most of all is you three!"

The End

Twirling Princess

Can you help Rapunzel with this dancing puzzle?

1

a

b

c

2

One of the pieces does not belong to the picture. Which one?

Match the jigsaw pieces to fit the spaces in the picture.

1

2

3

4

Answers on page 66.

24

Adventurous Rapunzel

Colour this picture of Rapunzel using the dots to help you.

All About ... Snow White

🍎 **Snow White is special because:** she is kind, fair, trusting and cheerful. Always happy to look after others, her friends love Snow White dearly in return.

🍎 **Snow White's special friends:** the Seven Dwarfs (Happy, Sneezy, Sleepy, Grumpy, Doc, Dopey and Bashful).

🍎 **Snow White's special love:** the Prince.

🍎 **A special moment in Snow White's story:** All of Snow White's friends are delighted when, after eating a poisoned apple and falling into a deadly sleep, she is awakened by the Prince giving her 'love's first kiss'.

Snow White is always busy
cooking and cleaning.
What useful jobs do you do at home?

🍎 Tidy my toys ☐✓

🍎 Set the table ☐✓

🍎 Feed my pets ☐✓

🍎 Help with the shopping ☐✓

🍎 Water the plants ☐✓

"Remember, you're the one who can fill the world with sunshine."

Snow White

Snow White's Story

Snow White is telling the forest creatures a story.
Look at the picture closely, then answer the question.

Which of these close-ups is not part of the big picture of Snow White and the animals?

a

b

c

d

e

Answer on page 66.

Gentle Snow White

Snow White will look extra-pretty if you colour in this picture of her.

Princess Wishes

1 One hot summer day, while Snow White was feeding the birds from her castle window, something strange happened. One of the birds looked thirsty ...

2 ... so Snow White went to get some fresh water.

3 When she returned with the bowl of water, three magical letters had appeared on the windowsill!

Where did they come from?

4 The first letter read: Draw your wish here.

5 Snow White imagined a beautiful ballgown and drew it on the magical letter.

I wish for a pretty dress.

My wish came true!

6 When she finished the drawing, Snow White realised she was wearing the ballgown she had wished for. "How wonderful!" she exclaimed.

7 The second letter read: Wish for something to eat and draw it here. Snow White drew a fabulous cake and it immediately appeared out of thin air!

Only one wish left.

Now wish with all your heart!

8 The last letter said Snow White should wish for something with all her heart. Can you guess what Snow White drew?

9 She wished to be with the Prince and all of her friends. Within seconds of finishing her drawing, Snow White magically appeared at the Dwarfs' cottage.

10 Snow White laughed, "It was no fun having a pretty dress and a big cake but no one to share it with. You're the best family a princess could ever wish for."

It's your turn to draw a special wish now! It might be a kitten, new party shoes or something else.

All About ...
Palace Pets

Read about each of the palace pets, then colour in the heart next to the right answer.

1 Meet

This silky white puppy belongs to Cinderella. She was a present from Prince Charming.

Guess what Pumpkin loves most:

a. Dancing ♡   b. Sleeping ♡   c. Growling ♡

2 Meet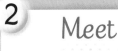

Ariel is this cute kitten's best princess friend. She adores swimming!

Treasure has red hair just like:

a. Prince Eric ♡   b. Ursula ♡   c. Ariel ♡

3 Meet

Snow White thinks this cute bunny is the sweetest of them all!

Berry loves hugs and:

a. Climbing ♡   b. Hopping ♡   c. Snoring ♡

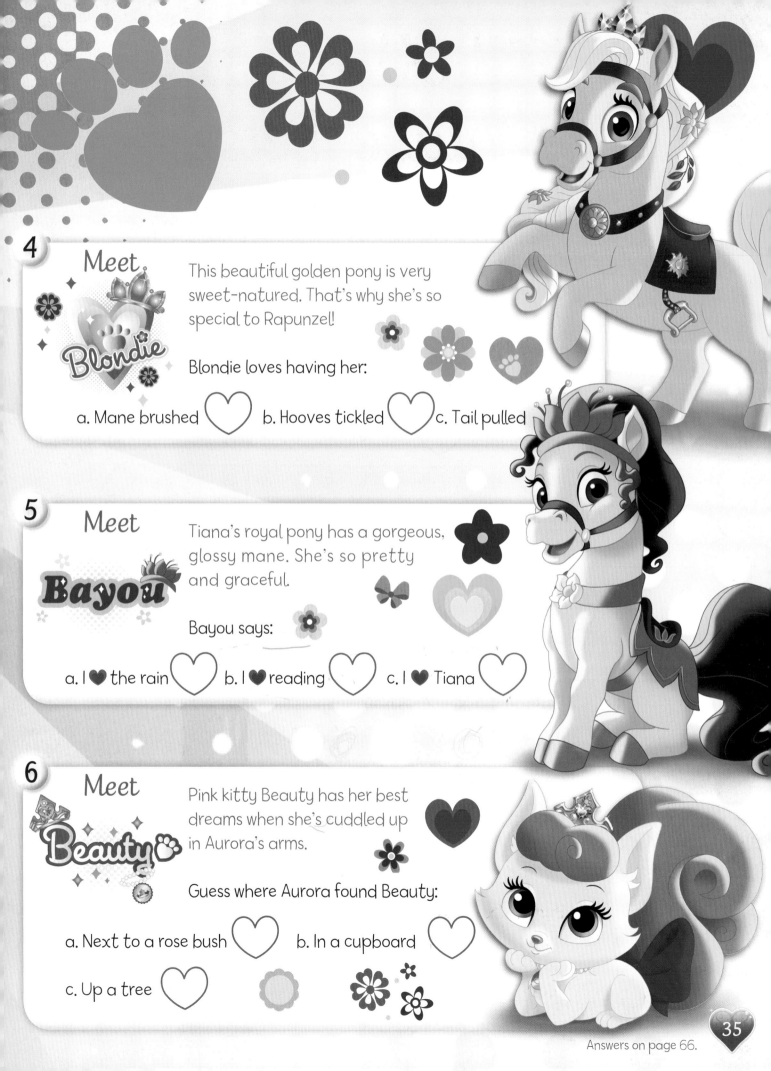

4 Meet **Blondie**

This beautiful golden pony is very sweet-natured. That's why she's so special to Rapunzel!

Blondie loves having her:

a. Mane brushed ♡   b. Hooves tickled ♡   c. Tail pulled

5 Meet **Bayou**

Tiana's royal pony has a gorgeous, glossy mane. She's so pretty and graceful.

Bayou says:

a. I ♥ the rain ♡   b. I ♥ reading ♡   c. I ♥ Tiana ♡

6 Meet **Beauty**

Pink kitty Beauty has her best dreams when she's cuddled up in Aurora's arms.

Guess where Aurora found Beauty:

a. Next to a rose bush ♡   b. In a cupboard ♡

c. Up a tree ♡

35

Answers on page 66.

Tidy and Find

The Palace pets are tidying up their belongings, but they've got in a muddle.

1

Every panel contains a necklace, perfume bottle, mirror, bowl and one other item. Can you circle the other item when you find it?

2

3

36

Answers on page 66.

Berry

Pumpkin

Cute and Sweet

Beauty

Missing Tiara

Pumpkin is brushed, dressed and almost ready to go to a royal ball, but she still needs to put on her tiara.

1

Can you help Pumpkin find her way through the maze of bows to her tiara?

2

Colour in the bows when you get there!

Answer on page 66.

All About ... Tiana

🌸 **Tiana is special because:** she is hopeful, bright, chic and kind. Tiana works hard to make sure her dream of opening a restaurant comes true.

🌸 **Tiana's special friends:** Charlotte, Louis (a trumpet-playing alligator) and Ray (a firefly).

🌸 **Tiana's special love:** Prince Naveen.

🌸 **A special moment in Tiana's story:** when Tiana and Prince Naveen are astonished to realise that they have both turned into frogs!

Trace over the letters below to
reveal the name of the restaurant
that Tiana opens.

Tiana's
Palace

Now think of three things you'd like to eat there!

1. sgobries

~~STRAWBERRIES~~
Strawberries

2. aPLos

apples

3. iys cream

ice cream

"If you do your best each and
every day, good things are sure to
come your way."

Tiana

Picnic Adventure

boat picnic basket Louis fireflies

Use these pictures to help you read this Tiana story.

Tiana and Naveen had planned a romantic picnic for themselves on the bayou. Naveen told Tiana to sit down and relax, while he peacefully rowed the . She let her hand run through the cool water as they drifted through a patch of water lilies. Then Naveen stopped and serenaded Tiana with a romantic song. The bayou frogs croaked right along with him. SPLASH! All of a sudden, Naveen and Tiana got a BIG surprise. the alligator popped up from the water and nearly tipped the over. Their flipped right into the swamp water! While Tiana and Naveen were happy to see , their romantic

picnic in the little  was ruined.

"Now don't you all worry," said Tiana.

"Supper can wait until we get home.

For now let's just enjoy this beautiful

setting." The three friends had a

wonderful time, but the sun was going

down and the bayou was soon so dark

that they couldn't find their way out!

Finally Tiana spotted some lights

winking in the distance.

"It's the !" she cried. With the

light from the , they were able to find

their way out of the bayou. pushed

as Tiana cuddled up next to Naveen. "My

picnic sure didn't turn out like I planned it,"

said Naveen. "But it was a perfectly

enchanting evening anyway ..." Tiana replied,

as she drifted off to sleep in Naveen's arms.

The
End

The Chef Princess

Tiana is trying out a new recipe for her restaurant.
Prince Naveen will taste it first!

Can you spot the 5 differences between the two pictures? Colour in a frog every time you see one.

1

2

44

Answers on page 66.

Tiana the Dreamer

Join up the dots, then colour in the dress to complete the picture.

1
2
3
4
5
6
7
8
9
10
11

45

Fashion Fun

There's a grand royal ball at the castle. Join in the excitement and help Tiana and the other princesses get ready.

1 Can you draw a line around the separate groups of perfumes, brushes, tiaras and slippers? We have found all the soaps.

2 Can you find this rose in the scene?

a

b

c

d

3

Which dress will each of the princesses change into for the ball? It is the same colour as the dress they are wearing now.

Answer on page 66.

47

All About ... Aurora

🌹 **Aurora is special because:** she is sweet, positive, elegant and thoughtful. She is always dreaming of one day finding true love.

🌹 **Aurora's special friends:** Flora, Fauna and Merriweather and the woodland creatures.

🌹 **Aurora's special love:** Prince Phillip.

🌹 **A special moment in Aurora's story:** when evil fairy, Maleficent, casts a spell on Aurora on her sixteenth birthday and sends her into an enchanted sleep.

Aurora loves to sing and play
with the creatures in the forest.
How many can you count in this picture?

There are ♡ creatures.

"If you dream a thing more than
once, it's sure to come true."

Aurora

Answer on page 66.

Pretty Crown

Make this sparkly crown. It's perfect for any princess!

Aurora says:
Use hair grips or elastic to make sure your princess crown stays in place.

You will need:

- pink card
- scissors
- sticky tape
- pencil
- glue
- jewels
- feather fabric
- glitter glue

Adult help needed.

1 Draw and cut out a crown shape from pink card.

2 Decorate the crown with feather fabric, glitter glue and jewels. Leave to dry.

3 Bend the crown into a circle so that the edges meet, then tape them together.

Aurora's Song

Will Aurora be brave enough to sing at the royal concert?
Listen to this story and find out.

Aurora often sang happily to herself and one day it gave the two kings a wonderful idea. "Please will you sing for us at our special royal concert?" they asked, excitedly.

Before Aurora could say a word, the kings had invited all of their friends.

"I don't think I can sing in front of such a big crowd," Aurora told Prince Phillip.

"You could practise away from the palace until you feel ready," suggested Prince Phillip. Aurora thought that this was a great idea, so they rode to a quiet part of the forest. Soon, Aurora's pretty voice filled the forest.

As Aurora practised, the creatures who lived in the forest came to listen. The birds sang and the animals chirruped and squeaked with joy. "Bravo!" cheered Prince Phillip. "You'll be note perfect tomorrow."

The next day, the palace welcomed all of the wonderful guests who had come for Aurora's concert. There must have been at least one hundred princes and princesses in the crowd!

Aurora felt so nervous that she couldn't remember how her song started! For a moment she just stood still. Everyone in the audience held their breath in anticipation.

Just then, the forest birds and animals came to the rescue. They squeaked, chirruped and whistled the song with Aurora and magic seemed to fill the air.

Aurora's song was so beautiful that everyone joined in. It was a wonderful way to spend the day and everyone loved Aurora's performance.

"Whenever I need help, my friends are always there," Aurora told the Prince, as he congratulated his talented princess.

The End

Hungry Horse

After taking Aurora for a ride, her horse is ready for a tasty snack.

1 Can you help Aurora find the right way through the maze?

Start

a   b   c

2 How many horseshoes can you count?

Finish

54

Answers on page 66.

Playful Aurora

Use your best colouring pens for this pretty picture of Aurora.

All About ... Ariel

🐚 **Ariel is special because:** she is adventurous, pretty, mischievous and free-spirited. Ariel takes brave risks to follow her dream of exploring the human world.

🐚 **Ariel's special friends:** Flounder (a fish), Sebastian (a crab) and Scuttle (a seagull).

🐚 **Ariel's special love:** Prince Eric.

🐚 **A special moment in Ariel's story:** when Ariel rescues Eric from a stormy sea and sings to him as he lies recovering on the beach. Once she returns to her underwater world, he has just the memory of her beautiful voice.

Ariel loves to wear shell jewellery.
Can you design a shell necklace,
especially for Ariel?

"I believe in discovering the
beauty in the world around me."

Ariel

Twins Everywhere!

Ariel loves the idea of having a twin. Today, she's playing with lots of twins under the sea!

Can you find all the twins in the picture? Draw a line to connect each pair, then colour in a heart.

Answers on page 66.

Fun-Loving Ariel

Colour in Ariel's hair and dress so that she looks perfect!

A Holiday at Home

1 One day, Ariel was exploring the ocean looking for human treasures. She couldn't believe her luck when she found a postcard floating on top of the sea.

2 On the front there was a picture of lots of people having fun at the beach. On the back, a handwritten message read: Wish you were here! xxx

Postcard

Wish you were here! x x x

3 "Holidays look like so much fun," thought Ariel, as she gazed at the postcard. "I wish I could go on one." She decided to ask her father when she got home.

4 King Triton laughed at Ariel's request. "Go on holiday!" he boomed. "What a silly idea! Who would protect the Kingdom from Ursula, the sea witch, if we went on holiday?"

5 Ariel's sisters had overheard King Triton. They felt sorry for Ariel. "I wish there was something we could do," sighed Attina.

6 "Maybe there is!" cried Arista. "If Ariel can't go away on holiday, why don't we bring a holiday to her?"

7 Ariel was surprised when, a little while later, Alana pulled up alongside her in a seahorse-drawn carriage. "Come aboard!" Alana cried. "We're off on holiday!"

61

8 "Wow!" Ariel gasped, as she arrived at the underwater beach her sisters had made for her. "Happy holiday!" they cheered, as Aquata handed Ariel a refreshing drink.

9 Ariel had lots of fun but eventually it was time to leave. "Don't forget to send a postcard home first!" said Andrina, handing Ariel a postcard.

10 Ariel used a conch shell filled with octopus ink to write a message on her postcard. Then Andrina stuck a tiny starfish on as a stamp. Ariel giggled as a dolphin took the postcard and swam away to deliver it.

11 When Ariel arrived home, King Triton was waiting for her. "Sorry I said you couldn't go on holiday," he told her. "It sounds like you had fun. Can I come next time?"

12 "Of course you can!" said Ariel. "Although next time I'd like to go to a city." Her sisters laughed. "Ariel the adventurer!" said Attina. "She always wants to try something new!"

The End

Postcard
Wish you were here!
Ariel
Atlantica

Postcard
Wishing you a great summer!
Ariel
Atlantica

Postcard
Let's go swimming
Ariel
Atlantica

Postcard
Having a whale of a time
Ariel
Atlantica

Who has Ariel written postcards to? Match the colour of the starfish stamps to the circles and find out who will get each card!

Who's Home First?

Which princess will get home to her palace first?
Play this game with a friend and decide who wins the race!

Lucifer is up to his old tricks again. Move back one.

Mother Gothel blocks your way. Move back one.

Miss a go to dance with the Dwarfs.

Your stepsisters trick you. Move back one.

Paint a picture of Pascal. Miss a go.

You get lost in the forest. Move back one.

Lady Tremaine gives you a chore. Miss a go.

Swing through the trees using your hair. Move forwards one.

The animals lead you on your way. Move forwards one.

Fairy Godmother helps you. Move forwards one.

Flynn keeps you waiting. Move back one.

You stop to kiss the Prince. Miss a go.

You need a counter for each player and a die. Each player chooses a princess. Take it in turns to throw the die and move the number of spaces along your princess's path. The first princess to reach her palace wins!

Firefly Ray glows to light your path. Move forwards one.

You have made Maleficent angry. Move back one.

Ursula sends you in the wrong direction. Miss a go.

You listen to Louis playing a tune. Miss a go.

The three fairies use their magic. Move forwards one.

You find a beautiful shell. Move back one.

Dr Facilier plays an evil trick. Move back one.

You play with this rabbit. Move back one.

You hear Eric calling. Move forwards one.

Prince Naveen can't find you. Move back one.

Prince Phillip kisses you. Miss a go.

Flounder has a secret to tell you. Move back one.

Answers

Pages 10-11: Garden Games
1) a – Gus, b – Lucifer, c – Jaq, d – Prince Charming, e – Bruno.
2) False, True, False.

Page 16: I Believe …
Cinderella's message is: 'wishes come true'.

Page 20: Bunny Friend
1) 9.
2) Pascal is by the flowers.

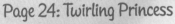

Page 21: Cute Pascal!
1) Picture a is different.
2) Pascal

Page 24: Twirling Princess
1) a – 3, b – 1, c – 4.
2) Jigsaw piece 2 does not belong.

Page 28: Snow White's Story
Close-up c is not part of the main picture.

Pages 34-35: All About … Palace Pets
1 – a, 2 – c, 3 – b, 4 – a, 5 – c, 6 – a.

Page 36: Tidy and Find
1 – saddle, 2 – bow, 3 – tiara.

Page 39: Missing Tiara

Page 44: The Chef Princess

Pages 46-47: Fashion Fun
2) The rose is on the back of the chair.
3) Snow White – c, Tiana – d, Aurora – a, Rapunzel – b.

Pages 48-49: All About … Aurora
There are 8 creatures.

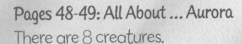

Page 54: Hungry Horse
1) Path c is correct.
2) 10.

Page 58: Twins Everywhere!

DISNEY PRINCESS

The Royal Palace hereby declares that:

ho No No

Write your name here.

has become a perfect princess.

She has shown that she is:

- friendly and kind

- bright and playful

- generous and loving

CONGRATULATIONS!

Stick or draw a picture of yourself here.

Disney
PRINCESS

Have you seen Disney Princess magazine?

Available at all good newsagents and supermarkets

Out every 2 weeks!